THE RABBIT'S ARROWS

K. J. PUGH

ISBN: 9798756612769

Artwork by Andrew Bosley (www.BosleyArt.com)

Graphic Design by Dann May (www.DannMay.com)

Audiobook by Michael J Tinker (www.MichaelJTinker.com)

Audiobook Music by Nicholas Alexander (www.NicholasAlexander.org)

FOR LYNN

Whose love sweetens my life,
Whose laugh enlivens my home,
Whose fellowship warms my soul,
And whose joy magnifies my own.

(www.StoriedTraveling.com)

AND FOR GRACE CHURCH, BOROUGBRIDGE

Who introduced us to the beauties of North Yorkshire,
Who welcomed us while foreigners,
And without whom this book would not exist.

(www.GraceChurchBoroughbridge.co.uk)

Read-Aloud Adventures publishes highly-localised adventure tales, combining imaginative storytelling with real-world places your family can visit and enjoy together. Each section of this story can be read aloud in roughly ten minutes, making it ideal for bedtime reading. In order to preserve a strong sense of place, all editions of this book (including the American edition) intentionally retain the Anglicised spellings of the story's setting.

Books in this Series:

The Rabbit's Arrows

The Mice of Marly-le-Roi

(www.ReadAloudAdventures.com)

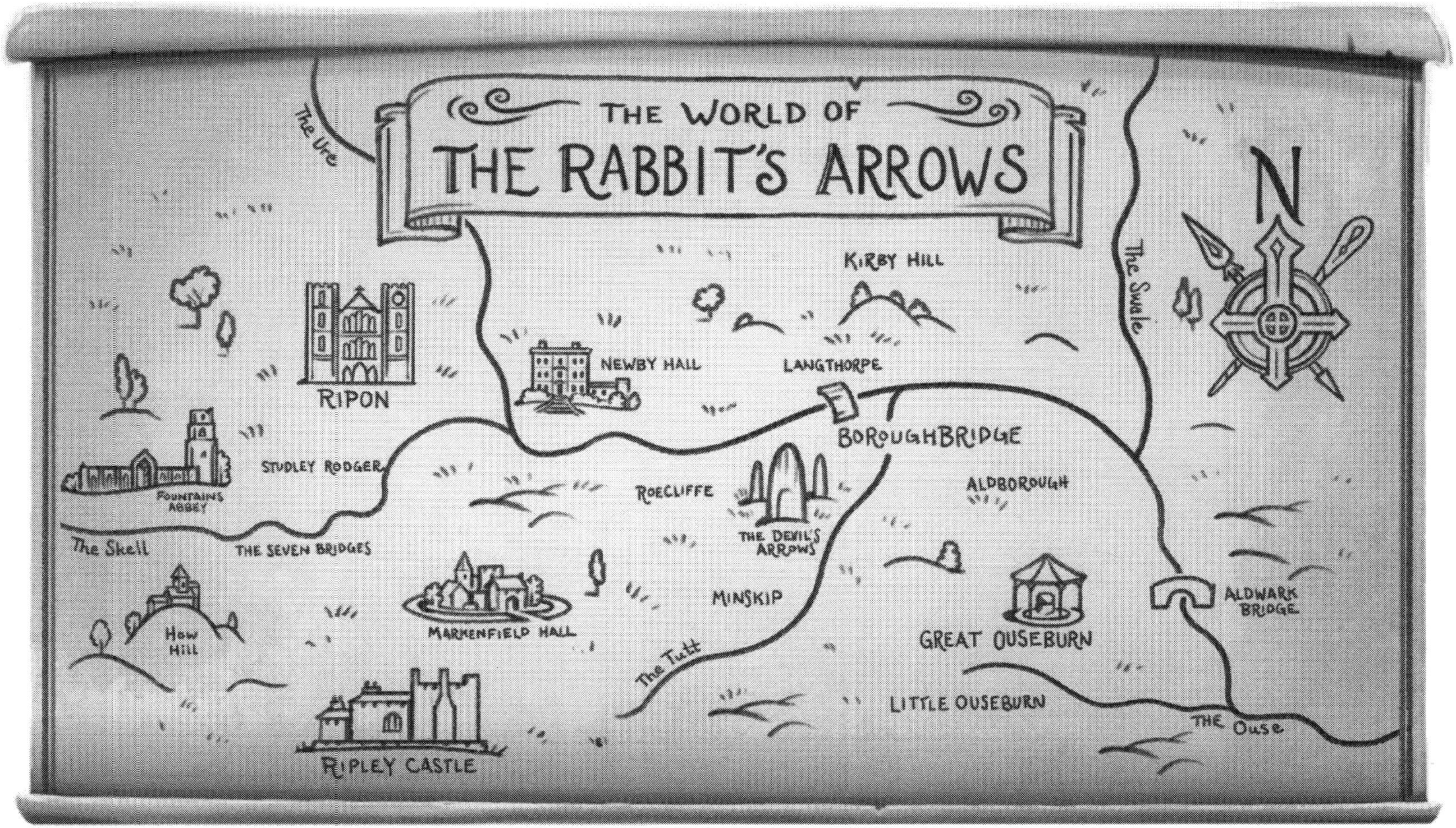
THE WORLD OF
THE RABBIT'S ARROWS
N
The Ure
The Swale
The Skell
The Tutt
THE Ouse
RIPON
FOUNTAINS ABBEY
STUDLEY RODGER
THE SEVEN BRIDGES
How Hill
MARKENFIELD HALL
RIPLEY CASTLE
NEWBY HALL
KIRBY HILL
LANGTHORPE
BOROUGHBRIDGE
ROECLIFFE
THE DEVIL'S ARROWS
MINSKIP
ALDBOROUGH
GREAT OUSEBURN
LITTLE OUSEBURN
ALDWARK BRIDGE

"Let me tell you a secret," the old man said between coughs. His hands shook like two wind-battered branches holding tightly to a cup of Yorkshire Tea.

"Come closer, lads," he said. We took another cautious step forward—feeling a discomfort not very unlike stepping too close to a blazing fire.

"Closer," the man wheezed, "A tad closer."

We leaned in as near as a timid child might when placed upon the lap of Father Christmas for the first time.

"Ahhhh-Choooww!" The man sneezed violently and right in our faces. He made no apologies, and none were expected—we were in rural North Yorkshire after all. And, here in God's own country, whatever doesn't kill you only serves to make you stronger. Or so the born-and-bred Yorkshiremen are fond of saying.

"I'll let you in on a secret, lads." The man leaned forward again as our spittle-speckled faces retreated a step back. He wiped his nose with a dirty handkerchief before continuing on in a near whisper.

"Everyone you know's blind," he said, his voice now beginning to rise. "Blind to what's right before their eyes, and the worst of it is that they poke fun at them that can see!" The man waved his hands about as he spoke, not caring how much tea went flying as long as he could make his point.

"But you two boys are still young enough, I'll wager. I was about your age when my eyes were first opened . . . to see the world as it really is. You won't believe what I'm about to tell you, but just you remember now how you found me."

How could we ever forget?! My friend Michael and I had found the man about an hour earlier face down in the dirt. He was covered in scratches from head to toe. His tired, tweed coat was full of jagged rips and old patches torn loose. He looked like a man who had been in a fight with a barbed wire fence and lost, quite badly.

The man's appearance, however, wasn't what stopped us in our tracks. The figure lying face-down on the path was surrounded by at least three dozen rabbits—all standing as tall as they might on their hind legs, as though they were watching over him.

"You remember how those rabbits refused to move a muscle until you two got me to my feet again?"

Our two heads nodded in agreement. What bunch of rabbits wouldn't run for cover with two heedless boys stomping down the path? If you're asking yourself that question, we did too. And our strange host knew it.

"Aye, that's troubled you, hasn't it? Well, there's much more to those rabbits than your wildest dreams might grant them. How old are you both? Nine . . . ten?"

We were both thirteen at the time, but he coughed so long and loud that he couldn't make us out as we answered.

"Well, no matter!" he said, after coughing through our third attempt to correct him. "I was about your age when I first walked the Ley Line marked by those stones." His hand pointed out the front door of his one-room house and down the path we'd helped him along, but we had no need to look back. We knew exactly what 'those stones' were. There were three of them, as tall as trees standing upright in a farmer's field. They were called *The Devil's Arrows* and got their name from an old tale. Locals told the story of how the Devil had a tiff with the ancient Roman town of Aldborough and threw these stone missiles at the town in his wrath. But stones thrown in anger often go amiss. The Devil missed his mark, and the stones stuck fast on the western outskirts of

Boroughbridge. Or so the story goes.

"You know the story of those stones?" Michael and I nodded and started to tell it.

"It's a pack of lies!" the man interrupted with a frantic wave of his hands that sent streams of tea flying.

"Yes, because the Devil . . ." I began.

"Because the Romans . . . !" he interjected again—this time with a cough. "Because when the Romans first arrived those stones had already been standing there for nearly three thousand years. A pack of lies that story is!"

"Oh," Michael said in his best schoolboy tone, "And I suppose *you* know the true story then, do you?"

The old man smiled, "Well, yes. I know something *more true*, at least." He leaned forwards and his raspy voice became a whisper again. "Those stones . . . listen closely, mind you! . . . those stones were set up by the first peoples ever to live on this island—the original Yorkshiremen, you might say. They set up those stones in order to mark an ancient Ley Line."

Vhat's a Ley Line?" I asked.

What's a Ley Line?" he repeated back. "Don't they teach anything useful in schools these days? You'll be asking me next, 'What's a compass? Or what's a map?' I'll bet!" He had to work his way through a wheezing laugh before he could continue on again.

"A Ley Line is a path as ancient as the land itself. It's not made by men, but a man might discover it by accident. If walked correctly, at the right time and on the right day, you'll find it quite the eye-opening experience, let me tell you! You'll be given what the Druids called *the Sight*—the ability to see what's really going on in the world around you."

He paused and looked searchingly into our eyes—as though he were inspecting eggs that might have passed their going-off date.

"Or perhaps," he reflected, "it's more correct to say that something rotten is burned out of your sight instead of anything extra added. I'm guessing that it has to happen before you reach a certain age—like washing up a dirty saucer before the scum hardens." The man appeared not to have washed a dish in quite some time from a glance around his place. The house looked much more like a lived-in workshop complete with sawdust on the floor and odd-looking tools scattered around.

"Whatever the case," he continued, "you can now see things that you've always been blind to before."

"Like what?" Michael asked.

"Like a war!—an unseen war that's raging all around us. You thought it was all 'survival of the fittest' and 'food chains' outside your door, I'll wager. Those are simple-minded explanations designed to make school children yawn and look the other way. I've seen what's really going on out there in wood, field and dale."

"What've you seen?" I asked, half wanting to hear but also half afraid of the answer. He took a long sip of tea and an even longer look out of the window, before locking eyes with us again.

"I've seen a squadron of falcons fly with more precision and planning than the Royal Air Force ever could. I've held in my hands the building blueprints of beavers and seen the amazing structures they hide in plain sight. I've overheard the secret war councils held by foxes. And . . ." he paused again, staring into our faces, "I've been a guest in the Halls of the Rabbit King."

"Surely you're making all this up," we protested. "Beavers don't make blueprints. Foxes don't hold war councils, no more than rabbits have kings. We're not so simple as to believe all that rot!"

The old man laughed, "If I only had 20 pence for every time someone told me that—why I could remodel this shack into a proper house!" He laughed again, but it wasn't the kind of laugh others want to join in. It was the sad laugh of a thousand disappointments.

"Still, I can't blame you for doubting me. I once saw things exactly the same as you do. But that was before. Before the day I walked the Ley Line at The Rabbit's Arrows—that's their proper name, by the way. Those stones out there have much more to do with rabbits than the Devil. Besides, there used to be four of them, like two pairs of giant rabbit ears poking above the ground—before some fool of a farmer pulled one down to bridge the River Tutt. The path of the Ley Line must've been clearer at one time. I imagine the four stones served like the sights of a gun, pointing straight down the line. With one stone missing, the true path is a bit harder to guess.

But finding the true line to walk is not nearly as hard as walking it on the right day and at the right time. I only remember that it was close to sunset when it happened to me. Like you, I was about eight or nine."

I began to correct him again, but Michael gave me a nudge and a look that said, "Don't bother. It's not worth it, mate."

"There wasn't much for kids to do in Boroughbridge in those days . . . which is another way of saying there was everything to do! I explored nearly every inch of the town as well as the villages—Roecliffe, Aldborough, Minskip, Langthorpe, Kirby Hill—I knew them all like the back of my hand by the time I was your age.

I knew every curve of the River Ure, from the Ripon Locks to the Aldwark Bridge. At Newby

Hall, we'd cross the river on homemade boats just to play hide-and-seek with the gardeners. Now, those were the good ol' days!" The old man laughed again, but the tone was different this time. It was the infectious laugh of childhood, which is never more than a memory away.

"I explored every bit and backwater around Boroughbridge, but those Arrows drew me back again and again like a ball on a string. I would often find myself gazing at them just before sunset, when it was time to turn towards home.

Then, the fateful day came. I was walking between the Arrows, when the light of the setting sun caught me full in the face. It was like turning a corner and suddenly meeting a car with its lights on full beam. The flash of light stopped me in my tracks, and suddenly I felt quite dizzy.

'Oh crumbs!' I remember saying to myself as I squatted down among the rows of barley. Only heaven knows how long I sat there nursing my head before a sudden rustle made me look up. In amazement, I rubbed my eyes once and then a second time.

There, standing on his hind legs in front of me, was a rabbit decked from ear to tail all in armour. Not the clunky kind you'd find on display at Markenfield Hall or Ripley Castle—this stuff was form-fitting and sleek—it moved effortlessly with the rabbit. Or, perhaps, it's fairer to say the rabbit moved effortlessly because he wore it.

'Now, who put that on you?!?' I said aloud, and the rabbit gave a sudden start. He took one bound away down the path and then froze—rooted to the spot. Slowly he turned his head and looked me over, as though it was his turn to be amazed. In that moment, I caught a glimpse of something in his eyes—

something I knew that I'd seen many times before but now seemed strangely out of place. As the rabbit turned full round, I saw the glint of a sword hanging at its side. While the two of us stared at one another, it suddenly dawned on me what foreign thing had found its way into those animal eyes. It was a human intelligence, swift and cunning.

In the same instant the rabbit must've come to his own conclusions about me, because, in one fluid motion, he leapt the distance between us and drew his sword. I scrambled backwards with feet and hands ploughing up the mucky field, but it was no use. In a split second, he landed with a thud on my chest and held the point of his sword to my throat.

'What . . . did . . . you . . . say?' The rabbit spoke slowly but with perfect clarity.

'You can talk!?!' I said, dumbfounded.

'You can both hear me and . . . see this sword?'

When no immediate response followed, he gave the top of my head a swat with the sword's blunt side. Whack!

'OUCH! Yes, I can see the sword and feel it too!'

'Answer this question quickly now or you might feel it again. Am I the first?'

'The first what?' I asked.

'The first you've seen . . . the first animal you've seen armoured for war?'

'This is ridiculous!' I said, attempting to push myself up.

'Answer the question.' He spoke with a firm tone resting the point of his blade upon the tip of my nose.

'Yes, of course, you're the first! And I can't believe I'm talking to you now. Oh dear, my head hurts . . . and not just from the knock you gave me!'

'Then you haven't chosen a side?'

'A side? A side in what?'

'A side in the war, of course.' I shook my head in response, and he gave me another appraising look. I could see the gears of his mind rapidly turning.

'In that case,' he said, 'let's start again.' He made something of a bow as he sheathed his sword, all while still standing on my chest.

'I'm Tobin,' he said, extending a furry paw to me. I could only stare back at him, completely at a loss. The rabbit made a face as though he were reconsidering how to proceed.

'Or . . . maybe you'd prefer as the southern hares do?' The rabbit withdrew his paw, and then awkwardly bent forward brushing his whiskers first against one of my cheeks and then again against the other.

'There now, that's done!' he said as one greatly relieved to have some unpleasantness behind him. 'It's customary to give your name in return.'

'Samuel,' I said, 'my name is Samuel, but my mates call me Little Sam, on account of me being a head shorter than the other Sam in my year. Do you know what they call him?'

'I'm sure I'll never guess,' the rabbit replied.

'Large Sam.'

I can still remember the first twitch of Tobin's whiskers as a laugh slowly worked its way out of him, 'Ha! An aptly named boy, I have no doubt. But all of your kind deserve the name *large* to me!'

Like a sudden flash, Tobin bounded off my chest. 'Follow me,' he said. 'I know of something large made just for you, Little Sam.' Without looking back, the rabbit cut a path through the barley straight for the smallest of The Devil's Arrows."

Even though this stone was the shortest of the three, it still towered over me like the imposing drawbridge of a sleeping giant's castle. If I could stand on my own shoulders six times over, I'd still fail to reach the top.

'Take a closer look, Little Sam,' Tobin said motioning towards the stone, 'and tell me what you see.'

At first I only saw the deep, weather-worn grooves running down the old stone, which to me have always seemed slightly akin to the first pass of a cheese grater down the side of an enormous potato. I began to ask the rabbit what I should be looking for when I saw it the unmistakable outline of a door.

'Yes, you can see it now. I bet you couldn't before today,' Tobin said. 'Hmmm, I wonder . . .

what might happen were you to trace your finger around the outline of the door?'

'I've always felt rather silly tracing things,' I objected as I began.

'I bet you've always felt silly talking to animals before too,' Tobin replied with a wink. 'One day many of the silly things will prove to be quite serious, Little Sam, and many of the serious things quite silly.'

As he spoke, my finger completed its journey tracing around the man-sized door. A loud click suddenly resounded from within the stone.

'What was that?' I said, as the initial click gave way to a low rumbling. The traced portion of rock began to sink into the ground like a slowly opening mouth, revealing a set of stone steps going down into the earth.

'I'm actually relieved that this door still works,' Tobin said. 'It has been ages since this way was last opened by a human hand. As you can tell, we rabbits prefer to use the holes instead. Far less dramatic of an entrance, if you ask me.'

I stood there peering down the steps, something

like an uneasy doctor peering down a sick child's throat.

'I don't know if I want to go down. It looks awfully dark.'

'Come now,' Tobin reproached, 'you stand on the brink of a great adventure.'

'I doubt that I'm old enough for any great adventures,' I said.

'Perhaps we rabbits reckon our age differently, but you don't appear too young to me! Just ask yourself this: when you've grown much older and lie dying upon some feathery bed (yes, we've looked into your windows at night and know how you humans sleep), what will you wish you had done?'

'You've looked through my bedroom window . . . while I was sleeping!'

'Well, perhaps not your window. But there are eyes upon you at all times, have no doubt. And not all of them are good and friendly. That's why we need you, Sam.'

'You need me, Tobin? May I call you Toby?'

'Yes, we need you. And, no, Sam. You may

NOT call me Toby.'

'Well, I guess I've seen too much to go back to my old life now.'

'Truly,' Tobin said. 'And you're about to see much more.'"

"Tobin was right, of course. I would see much more. I would see both moments of far greater wonder and far greater danger. But even so, I still vividly remember taking those first steps down into the realm of the Rabbit King—and the sense of dread that grew in the pit of my stomach.

As I descended under the cool earth, the light from the stone doorway at my back became more and more faint. No sooner had my foot left the last step then I heard an even louder *CLICK*, and the stone began to rise up again behind me. Before I could say, 'Uhhh, I'll just bob back home for my torch,' the way was shut with a heart-stopping *THUD*.

For one terrible moment, fear coursed through me like an electric current. Had I been tricked? Had I been trapped? You can live your whole life and never have any real cause to fear being buried alive. But in that moment, I feared never seeing the sun again.

'Courage, Little Sam,' said Tobin. 'Breathe deep. Let your eyes adjust. And look for the door. It's quite large . . . and perhaps a bit thicker than you are. It was made by one of your lot donkey's years ago.'

I tried to steady myself—slowly exhaling my fear with each new breath. Holding my arms out in front of me, I waited for my eyes to adjust enough to see them. Perhaps there was still a little light to be had from a rabbit hole here or there. When things no longer appeared as black as pitch, I began to move forwards with my hands outstretched.

'That's it. You're almost there. Now, just reach out and find the door latch."

I remember the feeling of ancient iron under my fingers. My hands ran over it again and again in increasing desperation looking for the latch. Panic rose in me with each failed attempt. Never before have I so wanted a door to open.

'Steady on . . . that's the latch in your right hand, there. Easy now, don't rush it . . . now you're stepping on my foot . . . *ouch,* get off!' Tobin exclaimed as the door finally gave way, and the two of us tumbled through tangled together.

I'll tell you—it was as though I'd stepped through the looking glass and fallen into another world altogether. That's the way any stranger would've felt too, falling into the Halls of the Rabbit King.

To my surprise, the hall was full of warm light—from where it came I never could tell. It had all the warmth and pleasantness of firelight, but without the smell of smoke or flicker of flame. My ears immediately drank in the rich sound of pipe and drum, and my body felt the thump of a dance coursing through the floor. Rabbits of differing sizes and hues filled the cavernous hall and its many side burrows. Those at the centre, before the throne, moved together to the rhythm of the music. Theirs was a dance that felt as old as life itself.

Upon a throne of red stone sat the Rabbit King.

He was the biggest rabbit I had ever seen, all dressed in regal colours of purple and gold. A precious stone was bound to his brow, fastened by silver bands that ran around his greying ears. He sat mostly upright reclining upon fur pillows with his head slightly tilted back—completely and contentedly asleep.

Several of the rabbits in the hall were decked out in armour similar to Tobin's, but additionally many of them wore sashes of royal colours. Nearly all of these were carrying short pikes—the points of which, oddly enough, looked rather like carrots.

These guards were stationed along the many tunnel entrances to the hall. But at the sight of us falling through the door, many of them abandoned their posts and rushed towards us, spears at the ready. Other guards mustered around the sleeping king. Here and there about the hall, rabbits dressed in other fine colours drew swords and gathered their more vulnerable kin behind them. The music in the hall came to a crashing stop.

By the time we made it to our feet again, nearly two dozen pikes were pointed up at me. If it was possible to feel fear in that cosy place, I came close to feeling it. But wonder has the surprising side effect of driving out one's fears.

'Hear me!' Tobin cried, as he gracefully combined the act of dusting himself off with a courtly bow.

'This one has entered by the Guardian's Door into the King's Warren! His own finger traced and opened the Secret Stair. He has walked *the Line* and has received *the Sight,* just as those Guardians did in the tales of old! He calls himself . . . Sam.'

At this the old king stirred upon the red throne. He glanced from where we stood to his folk filling the warren about him, who were now whispering excitedly. A smile dawned upon his tired face as he looked back to us again. With a wave of his ringed paw the grip upon every pike and sword was relaxed, and the guards stood at ease.

'Beyond hope,' his clear voice rang out, 'a new Guardian arrives at our time of greatest need. This is the stuff of legends indeed.'

'I'm not the stuff of legends—you are!' I was tempted to shout back.

'But . . .' the King continued, 'possessing *the Sight* alone does not a true Guardian make. Let him first be tested. Only then will we permit ourselves to hope.'

Glancing toward a slender rabbit who was awkwardly wearing a monocle over one eye, the king spoke again. 'Venerable Archibald, please offer our guest *the cup,* if you will be so kind.'

'Yes, at once, my lord!' came the reply. From somewhere between his oversized overcoat and his undersized waistcoat, the Venerable Archibald produced a small jewelled cup. Every eye in the warren—a hundred rabbits or more—followed him as Archibald took the cup to the far side of the hall. There, coming out of the wall, was a flowing fountain that I had not noticed at first. It trickled down like a tiered waterfall into a pool that flowed along the whole length of the far wall. With a touch of ceremony, Archibald dipped the cup and carefully brought it over to where I stood. Paws extended, and with a slight bow of the head, he offered it up to me.

'What is this?' I asked.

'It's the Guardian's Cup,' Archibald replied in a reverent tone.

'It's polite to accept it,' Tobin added, looking up at me.

'Well, thank you.' I said taking it. A host of furry, expectant faces looked on as I drained the small vessel in one go. It tasted sweet and cool to the tongue, but it crawled down one's throat like a slow-moving forest fire—filling the body with a soothing warmth.

'Mmm, that's actually rather nice! Does it come in pints?' I asked with a laugh as I handed the cup back.

'No,' said a voice from the red throne, 'but it

does start you on a journey. Tobin, help him.' Tobin and the other rabbits gathered round as my legs began to give way under me. I felt my vision suddenly blur, as they eased me to the floor. The last thing I remember is Tobin saying in my ear, 'Embrace it like a sweet dream. I'll be watching over you as your journey begins, Little Sam.'

I woke up in the dark and the cold. For a second time fear gripped me. Was I locked away in some underground vault—tricked into being a prisoner of the Rabbit King? This worry washed over me until I saw them, like beautiful cracks in a prison's ceiling. My refocusing eyes caught sight of twinkling stars above me. I could make out whiffs of cloud now sailing across the starry sky as I lay on my back. Now, the top of one of the Arrows became clear as well.

'Was it all a dream?' I said to myself.

'No,' a voice spoke back. My chest pounded, as a dark head with two long ears now covered up part of the night sky above me.

'No, it was not a dream,' Tobin said just inches above my face. 'You've never been more awake.

Come tomorrow to Great Ouseburn—to the pavilion with the stone. Your first test begins there.'

'Great Ouseburn?' I repeated. 'Yes, I know the village . . . but why there?'

'Come tomorrow, and I will tell you more then,' Tobin replied. 'But this I will tell you now: the future of all you've seen, of the entire King's Warren may very well depend on you coming to Great Ouseburn tomorrow. So, please, do not fail us!'"

"Great Ouseburn is a village of just over one hundred families and double the size of its nearest neighbour—Little Ouseburn. The village sits near the source of the Ouse, an ambitious little stream which runs into the much larger River Ure and takes over the river's name from that point on. Other than a connection with Anne Brontë, there is not much remarkable to say about the village of Great Ouseburn . . . and that makes it *exactly* the kind of place where remarkable things are most likely to happen!

The next day I found myself off school and cycling towards Great Ouseburn at quite a clip. Whatever adventure had fallen into my lap, I decided to embrace it. After all, I'd made it through the day before without as much as a scratch. How much danger could I be in, really? I hadn't the foggiest idea, but I soon would.

My bicycle had only just come to rest beside the small pavilion at the village centre when I heard a '*Psssst!*' coming out of a nearby clump of tall grass. As Tobin raised himself up out of the weeds, I was again impressed by his skilfully woven armour. If the sun had been out that morning, I would've expected flashes off its silver plate to draw unwanted attention.

'Don't worry. Only you can see it,' Tobin reminded me. 'Besides all the humans have gone to their day-places by now. No one is about.'

Just as he said that, a lorry rounded the corner and drove down Branton Lane. Tobin brandished his sword and waved it around. I gave a half-wave and a sheepish grin as the lorry driver stared out his window at the two of us. He waved back but didn't slow down.

'See, I'm practically invisible to your lot. Now, have a look over there.' Tobin pointed his sword at the open air structure. The village's pavilion stood over a large stone, weighing a ton or two. The stone was raised up on several tiers of masonry—not looking at all remarkable.

'Why are we here for a stone?' I asked.

'It's not the stone we're here for. It's what the stone contains.'

'What's in it?'

Tobin shook his head. 'I'm afraid I can't tell you or help you in any way. This is *your* test. It's one thing to have *the Sight,* it's another to claim the weapon of a Guardian.'

'Oh, so it's a weapon then, is it?'

Tobin made a gesture with his ears—like he was locking his mouth and throwing away the key. I was on my own.

The stone (as I'm sure you boys know) is quite large with many surfaces. I began to study each of these like I've never studied anything in school. It wasn't until I stood up on the steps and was looking at the top that I saw something I hadn't noticed before—the outline of a box with writing inside it. Others can't see it. I've asked them since if they can. Seeing such inscriptions must only come to Ley Line Walkers, like myself. The inscription was written in large capital letters, *AS AT MERIBAH.*"

At this point, the old storyteller reclined back with his cup of Yorkshire tea, grinning and looking rather pleased with himself. "You two lads know what that means, right?"

Startled by the transition from an engaging story to an unexpected exam, Michael and I looked at each other and shook our heads, "No, how could we?"

"How could you know? Why, haven't you two ever been to Sunday School? A little knowledge of the ancient past often comes in mighty handy in the present day, I think you'll find."

We stared at him blankly for an awkwardly long period of time before Ol' Sam resumed with his story.

"Fortunately, *I had* been to Sunday School. So I'll tell you what the inscription meant, and what I did," our host continued. "Just as Moses struck the rock in the wilderness of Meribah in order to open it, so I struck the rock at Great Ouseburn. I hit it with my fist as hard as I could while saying in my most commanding voice, 'Open Up!' And do you know what happened?"

"What?" we asked.

"I nearly broke my hand." He laughed, "It's funny now, but I wasn't laughing much at the time. I was on the verge of giving up, when I looked imploringly at my little friend. Tobin smiled and above his head traced the outline of a box with his two ears, before repeating the lip-sealing gesture with a wink of his eye.

This time I ran my fingers around the box containing the inscription—just like I traced the door at the Arrows—and a bluish glow began to appear. Once the box's outline was complete, I again struck the stone dead centre. This time the stone cracked and fell in upon itself. Water began bubbling out of the top and running in all directions. A few seconds later, I saw it.

A staff of almond wood as tall as me floated up right before my eyes—almost like a cobra rising up out of a rock. Cascading down the shaft were blue, glowing braids of Druid design. Cautiously, I reached out and took it from the stone. The bluish glow began to retreat from where my hand grasped it. The staff shook internally with the feeling of a stampeding cavalry returning to its secret woodland stronghold. Even with all its magical light now faded, I knew that I held something of real power.

'Well done,' Tobin said as the stone resealed itself. 'You now possess *the Sight* and the Weapon of a Guardian. With this staff, you can protect the King's Warren from those who seek to destroy it. Remember always—this is the weapon of a protector, not a warrior. None now living know what it's truly capable of. Like you, it is the stuff of legend. A weapon to guard a flock from its enemies.'

Looking the staff over, I asked, 'What are these

enemies you keep going on about?'

'A rabbit has many enemies, Little Sam—the weasel, the stoat, the polecat, and some of the larger birds of prey, of course.' Tobin spoke now through gritted teeth, 'Our ancient and most crafty enemy, however, has always been the fox.'

'If you've always had these enemies, why did the Rabbit King say this was your hour of greatest need?'

'These enemies have always been ours, it's true, but we've always fought them off one at a time. Never before have our enemies set aside their differences and banded together against us. The foxen folk have somehow devised a way to bring all the Rabbit King's enemies together under one banner. Their combined strength would overwhelm all our defences—spelling the end of the King's Warren.'

We both stood for a moment in silence. The world already seemed a little less bright with the thought of no King's Warren in it.

'If there is anything I can do to stop that from happening, I will.'

'Thank you,' Tobin said. 'A Guardian with a staff is, indeed, a great cause for hope. But you will do us no good whatsoever if the battle comes while you're home in bed. We must know *when* the enemy plans their combined attack. And to know that, we must go to Ripon.'

'Why? What's in Ripon?' I asked.

'You have *the Sight* and the Weapon of a Guardian, but one thing is missing still.' He pointed at his ears. 'You need the Hearing of a Guardian as well. And for that, we must be off to Ripon Cathedral.'"

"I knew from experience that Ripon Cathedral was, even with the wind at your back, a good hour's ride from Great Ouseburn. Who knows how long it takes as the rabbit runs? So I offered Tobin a lift.

'A knight's dignity must bow to the pressing needs of the Warren,' he said as I picked him up like a sack of flour and placed him in my bicycle's front basket. But I dare say that my little friend enjoyed himself well enough. As we took the cut through Newby Hall, I even heard him say, 'I have always admired this place. If ever my King charters a new colony, here is where you'll find me.' Then he added with a sigh, 'It's a shame that expanding the Warren seems out of the question in such troubled times.'

'A shame, indeed.' I tightened my belt and pedalled faster.

We passed by the Ripon Races with the dates of its new season freshly painted on the wall. As I cycled beside the canal, we attracted a few odd glances from the city folk.

Ripon is, after all, a proper city. Do you know why, boys?" the old man asked, looking up from another long sip of tea.

"Yes," Michael said, "because it has a cathedral."

"Right you are, lad! I guess they do teach you something in those schools after all." The old man gave a wink and a laugh before continuing.

"Well, there we were at Ripon Cathedral, looking like a boy who had taken his pet rabbit out for a joyride. No one would have suspected us for a couple of sneak thieves about to pull off what would amount to the heist of the century!

'What's the plan?' I asked Tobin as we came to a stop and gazed up at the impressive arches and stained glass windows.

'We need to get into St. Wilfrid's Crypt under the cathedral. How would you suggest getting in?' He looked me over and frowned. 'I think tunnelling in may be a little out of the question.'

'How about the front door?'

'A bold plan, I like it.' Tobin said, patting the hilt of his sword in a way that resembled a cowboy patting his revolver.

Fortunately, we met no one at the door as we entered the cathedral. Otherwise, I'm not sure what Tobin might have done. He looked every bit the noble knight, while also seeming to possess the agility of a miniature ninja. I feared for the churchwarden who might get in Tobin's way. He didn't seem like the kind to sucker-punch a sexton in the throat while about his church business, but I was only just getting to know my little rabbit friend after all.

We snuck our way down a side aisle of the nave without anyone spying us. I pointed with my staff to the stairs leading down to the crypt. 'This way,' I whispered to Tobin.

We made our way down into the crypt—the oldest part of the cathedral—the only part to survive the Viking invasions which destroyed the original building above it. After navigating the narrow stone passageways, we came out in a small whitewashed room. There were a few recesses carved into the stone walls, but not much else. It could easily be the most unimpressive room in the world.

'Why are we here?' I asked, 'Or is this another test that I have to figure out by myself?'

'No, we're here to find what Wilfrid hid in this room for safekeeping. Do you know anything about him?'

'Only what the sign to the crypt says—that he lived and died back in the 600s.'

'If that's all you know, then we rabbits remember a lot more. Wilfrid was a man obsessed with the story of Ruby's Master . . . or at least that's what we call it. You know that story by another name, I believe.'

I could only raise my shoulders at a loss.

'If it helps, I believe the master's name was Balaam,' Tobin said, 'and Ruby is, of course, a donkey's name. The donkey saw the hidden danger in the way and spoke to her master, just like we're speaking now. I'm not sure, however, if any Ley Lines were involved in this particular case.'

'Oh, you mean the story of Balaam's donkey!' I said.

'Whose story it is depends on your perspective, I suppose,' Tobin added. 'Anyway, Wilfrid became obsessed with the story and with talking to animals in general. Somehow he created a *Helm of Hearing* that could pick up the speech of animals and also extend the wearer's hearing far afield. We'll need to find this (and fast!) if we're to discover the plans of the Rabbit King's enemies. Have a look around the room and see if anything strikes you as strange.'

'I can tell you one thing that is strange right away,' I said looking around. 'The symmetry of this room is way off.' I pointed to one of the recesses in the wall. 'If there is a little hollow space here on the left, wouldn't you expect a matching one here on the right as well? But it's oddly missing.'

As I said this, I began tracing with my finger where the other recess should have been. And do you know what happened? The now familiar bluish glow began to appear upon the stone. It continued to grow until it took the same form of the arched recess to the left of it.

'Do you think I should strike it with my fist?' I asked.

'Hmm. These sort of things seldom work the same way twice.' Tobin stroked his whiskers while looking around the room. 'Well, hello there . . . look at your staff now, Sam!'

I turned back to where I'd laid the staff against the wall. The almond wood head, which did look a bit like a cobra, began to radiate the same shade of blue.

'Now, that's interesting,' Tobin said, as I took up the staff and touched its head to the wall. Another bluish line grew outward from the point of contact, splitting the alcove into two doors. I gave a little push, and in response the two doors opened outward. There, upon a small pedestal in the recess, sat a helmet unlike any other I'd ever seen. It was mostly made of metal and fashioned to look like a pointy priestly hat. Imagine what the Pope might wear on his head if he rode out to war, and you'd be pretty close to it. The most striking aspect of the helmet was that on each side, almost like wings, there extended two large animal-like ears.

'How do I look?' I said putting it on.

'Ridiculous, of course,' Tobin replied. 'But at least now we're ready to face the real danger.'

'How's that, now? . . . The *real* danger, did you say?'

'Yes, the Fox's war council,' Tobin said. 'It's happening tonight!'"

"How Hill sits upon the southern side of Fountains Abbey, which is—as I'm sure you boys know—one of the most impressive ruins in all of England. Many a cathedral would feel more worshipful if its roof was the open sky and its floor the green grass like the abbey. You look up to ponder the infinite, and yet still feel free to run about and play like barefoot children. One feels the proper mix of hushed wonder and childlike joy in that place.

On How Hill, however, I've only ever felt fear. As the moon rose and the night drew in around us, Tobin and I arrived at the abandoned tower that rests atop the hill, like a jagged crown of grey stone. We chose this place because it afforded a clear view of the smaller, neighbouring hill to the south. Upon this smaller hill a solitary tree grows—like a lonely island amidst a blowing sea of barley. From our hiding place on How Hill, the tree was well out of bowshot (even for a Welshman!), but with Wilfrid's Helm I could hear everything that was happening around the tree—every squawk, every grunt, and every word.

'Hear me all!' said a sly voice, 'and let this war council make its start.' The murmur of many voices—some small and squeaky, others deep and harsh—gradually subsided until all was still and silent. The first voice continued, 'You've done well to come, Weasel and Stoat . . . Polecat and Hawk . . . along with my Fox kindred of the River and Dale.'

A great white fox slowly paced in a circle under the tree, stopping occasionally to bow in acknowledgement to each of the animal clans as he spoke. There were weasels, standing together on their hind legs, all in leathery armour and carrying a mix of spears and clubs. Next to them the stoats gathered, each carrying a pair of small, leaf-bladed daggers. Every so often, one stoat would toss a dagger whirling high into the air before catching it again. Beside these the polecats stood, each one looking eager for a fight—even if it was only among themselves. The hawks hung upon the tree branches, looking down on the proceedings with hungry eyes. All the other foxes present, except for their albino leader, had the red colour that you would expect in a fox. Unlike the war gear on the other animals, the foxes dressed richly as though they were going to a masquerade ball, not to a battle. Their only weapons were steel claws, attached like lethal extensions to each paw.

'We have gathered,' the White Fox continued, 'to do what none have been able to do before us—bring a final end to the King's Warren. Too long has the Rabbit King grown fat and his people withstood us while we stayed scattered and our strength divided. But no more! Together, in one swift stroke, we shall overcome them. By this time tomorrow, we will be dividing up all the hoarded wealth of the King's Warren.'

Some shouted aloud, 'Hear, Hear!' in response. But not all.

'How do we all know you'll do what's fair and

right by us?' said a large weasel who was pounding a rather cruel-looking club upon the ground as he spoke.

'Weasels are well known for their sense of fairness,' the White Fox said and everyone laughed in response, especially the weasels. 'You'll get all that is coming to you. My pack and I give you our word.'

'Ah, the word of a fox,' a polecat scoffed. 'I'm beginning to see why we've never attempted this before.'

'That's not the only reason,' came a shrill voice from up in the tree. 'Combining our power to destroy the King's Warren means a feast today, certainly. But what about tomorrow? Feast today, famine tomorrow, I say!'

With that a few other hawks took up the call, 'Feast today, famine tomorrow! Feast today, famine tomorrow! Squawk, squawk!'

'With all due respect to the wisdom of our flying friends,' the White Fox said with a bow towards the treetop, 'in taking the King's Warren, we destroy not our prey . . . but only their protector. Scattered and leaderless, the rabbit folk will be far easier to prey upon than they are now. Besides, we hear tell that the Halls of the Rabbit King are vast and full of many strong storehouses. Once we've emptied these for ourselves, I'm sure they'll make some splendid prisons for their former masters. Captive prey will taste just as sweet as those hunted down and hard won, I'll wager!'

This met with some loud grunts of approval, particularly from among the weasels and stoats. Tobin, however, tensed up with fury at these words.

'Can you hear all this too?' I asked in a whisper.

'Not as well as you can—which is a bit ironic—but I've heard enough to know now when the attack is coming. Things are happening even quicker than the Venerable Archibald foretold.'

Just at that moment, the war council went strangely silent—except, of course, for the sound of a hundred noses all sniffing the air at once. 'Can you smell that?' a fox cloaked in emerald green asked aloud.

'No, we can't!' came a unison of squawks from up in the tree.

'Hush!' said the White Fox. 'I smell it. It's human . . . and . . . rabbit . . . they're *together*. The wind has shifted. It's now coming from the North.'

With that pronouncement, every beady eye on and under the tree looked our way together. Atop How Hill my heart pounded in my throat.

'Hawks to air!' was the last thing I heard before pulling off Wilfrid's helmet.

'They're coming!' I said to Tobin, 'What do we do!?!'

'We must warn the Warren, and quickly!' The two of us bolted from our hiding place and ran straight for my bicycle hidden on the other side of the hill. Only as I reached it, did I look back to notice that Tobin was no longer at my side. He stood still and resolute, back at the base of the grey tower.

'I can't go with you,' he called out.

'What do you mean!?!'

'Someone has to stay behind.'

'Whatever for!?!' I cried.

'Trust me. They will never stop the pursuit until they catch someone. And the one that's caught can't be you . . . or else this war is lost before it's begun.'

'Tobin, no! Don't do this!'

'Don't stop until you reach the King's Warren. Farewell, my brave Sam!'

With those words, Tobin drew his sword and charged back in the direction of our pursuers. Before I could call out to him again, he was already lost to the darkness. Panic took hold as I mounted my bicycle and raced down the hill, pedalling hard towards Boroughbridge. I did not see a single pursuer the whole way home, but neither could I shake the feeling of being watched.

As I reached the outskirts of Boroughbridge, I abandoned my bike along Roecliffe Lane and ran across the farmer's field. Out of breath, I reached the smallest of the Arrows. As I began to trace the doorway with my finger, a single hawk alighted atop it.

'I've been waiting,' she said in a wispy voice. 'Do I have the honour of addressing a Guardian?'

'I can understand your speech and see that you're dressed for war, if that's what you mean.' In reply the hawk extended her wings backwards and bowed her head towards me.

'The White Fox wishes to meet you. Tomorrow at dawn, before the . . . um . . . the day's work he has planned.'

'And why should I ever want to meet him?' Tears came uncalled for as I thought of what the White Fox and his skulking pack might have done to the noble Tobin.

'Oh, I think you will want to meet him . . . if you ever want to see your rabbit friend again, alive and unspoiled.'

'Tobin! He's alright! Where is he?'

'Not far from where you left him. He put up quite the fight, that one! Some are now wondering if it will be as easy as the White Fox says to clean out this Warren. How many more fighters like him does the Rabbit King have? Some are now wondering.'

'Where is he?' I said again.

'Come to the valley of the Seven Bridges tomorrow, and you'll be sure to see him. Come alone, if you don't want to see him die.'

With those words, the lady hawk made one last bow before flying off into the night."

"The Seven Bridges, as you've probably noticed, is a bit of a misnomer. I have only ever found six bridges myself. Where the seventh bridge is, I do not know. No doubt finding the lost bridge is an adventure suited now for younger legs than mine.

The six bridges I have found, however, all cross the same little river. The River Skell runs like a snake through the narrow valley of the Seven Bridges, sometimes hugging one cliff side and sometimes the other. The oldest of the bridges are the most picturesque, built of grey and brown stone forming curved archways across the river. Imagine the kind of bridge that a romantic Victorian might build simply for the pleasure of looking at it, and you've probably got the right picture in mind.

The course of the River Skell through the valley roughly creates a set of small islands—bordered by rushing water on three sides and by a steep cliff on the one side that remains. If you're not an Olympian long jumper or uphill climber, then crossing the bridges remains your only way in or out of the valley.

All these features make the Seven Bridges a wonderful walk, but a hazardous battlefield. And a battlefield is exactly what it became.

The Battle of the Seven Bridges—it was my first time in a fight, you know. Oh yes, I'd punched a bully in the nose once before, but he only smiled and laughed at me in return. Nothing had prepared me for a real battle with life and death on the line—nothing, that is, except perhaps for a few good stories. Good stories of bravery and friendship in the face of certain danger, thankfully these were the bread and butter of my childhood. Without such stories driving me on, I don't know if I would've had the courage even to get dressed that morning.

But get dressed I did. I put on my thickest jumper, wanting a little extra protection from tooth and claw—not to mention the real weapons that I could now see. As I pulled my jumper over my head, I remember being happy that the thickest one I owned was red. 'If the enemy were to draw blood, you don't want them to see it,' I thought. 'Along those lines . . . I better get my brown trousers out of the wash as well.'

As the sun rose that morning, I rode out like a knight about to meet his destiny—if knights rode bicycles instead of horses, of course. With Wilfrid's Helm sitting atop my head and the almond wood staff strapped to my back, I cycled on until I was just outside the village of Studley Roger. It's actually more of a hamlet than a village—just a collection of a few houses resting on the back door of the Studley Royal Deer Park. Thankfully, the hour was still early and no one was yet stirring. Here I left my bicycle behind and began walking down the trail towards the Seven Bridges.

'What if things don't work out?' my doubts began to pester. 'You could turn back now, Sam, and none of your *real* friends—your human friends—would ever know anything about it.' My pace slowed as I wrestled with my thoughts.

'No, I can't turn back now!' I had to speak the words aloud to myself. 'Just because the fight is unseen, it doesn't make it unimportant. Besides, you're Tobin's only hope, Sam. Be brave for him.'

I walked down the trail now with increasing resolve as well as increasing certainty that I was being watched. The trees themselves seemed to have eyes, or at least they wilfully concealed other creatures who did. Even before I crossed the first bridge, I could see where my fate would be decided. Just beyond the next bend, hawks flew high encircling one another in a tornado-like spiral stretching far up into the sky. It felt like walking towards the eye of a storm . . . or into the centre of a trap.

As I turned the corner of the ridge, the White Fox's full army came into view. There were the weasels, all in armour and standing together like companies of spearman. The stoats stood together also, each hairy hand clutching small daggers and looking eager. The polecats were organised a bit more haphazardly upon each flank, acting like an outer shield protecting the main body. Most of the foxes stood together at the centre, although several of them were scattered among the others like captains over their companies. The White Fox took his place on the frontline, right at the river's edge. When I reached the place directly across the water from him, he spoke.

'Welcome, Guardian. It has been a long time since any of your kind have entered into our wars and played a part in our struggles for survival. Because that's exactly what this is, you know. It is *our* survival that's on the line, not yours. See these poor fellows with me,' the Fox said as he motioned to the weasels shaking their spears and the stoats pretending to sharpen their knives. 'They are only in this for their next meal, and I am only trying to help them find it. How can any son of man find fault with an old fox's care and compassion for his fellow creatures, I ask you?' With these words, the White Fox grinned as though he had already won, and many of the other foxes smiled with him.

'With compassion, there is no fault,' I answered back, 'but when your compassion looks like all-out war, then something is clearly amiss. If you're interested in survival, so am I. What about the survival of my friends? Where is Tobin?'

'Bring forward the troublemaker,' the White Fox sighed. In response, two of the larger foxes stepped forward with a rope between their mouths. From the rope hung Tobin, tied and suspended just above the ground. Even with his arms and torso bound tightly, he still thrashed about with his hind legs—almost landing a kick to the head of a nearby weasel.

'This one is far more trouble than he is worth. Nevertheless, I'd happily give him to you for a simple gesture of goodwill on your part.'

'What do you want?' I asked.

'Simply lay down your staff and that fancy helmet—it doesn't become you anyway. Then you can take your friend and go home. This is not your fight, after all. The age when animal-kind needed human Guardians is long past.'

'*Nooo!*' came a shout from the Fox's side of the river. It was Tobin. 'No, don't do it, Sam! I'd rather die here and now, than live on to see a Guardian give up the fight!'

'But I can't stand by and let you die, Tobin!' I shouted back.

'No, nor can we!' This time the voice came from my side of the river, and a great thudding and thumping was heard behind me like a distant stampede. Out of holes in the ground, out of fresh openings in the hillside, and rushing around the bend came a host of rabbits armed for war. They rushed forward down the valley like a bounding wave upon the beach. The wave came to an abrupt stop just behind me, quickly organising itself into rows and columns. Rabbits with pikes stood at attention, in lines of royal purple and gold. Other rabbits, sword in hand, wore the colours and devices of their houses—a green tree on the background of a silver moon, an orange carrot emerging from a pool of blue, three white pikes on a field of pitch black. These devices were shown proudly on their sashes and banners. But chief among them was the banner of the King's Warren—a golden crown on a purple plain atop three standing stones.

'For the King's Warren!' The shout went up as the last of the armoured rabbits found their places.

'For our brother-in-arms!' came a shout in return. Then every pike went pounding upon the ground and every sword upon shield. The clamour would've stirred the blood of the most peace-loving man who heard it.

Surprisingly, however, the White Fox's only response was to snicker.

'Ha, ha, ha! Well done! We rather hoped you all would be joining us. You've spared us an awful lot of trouble by doing so.'

With that the loud cry of a bird was heard, and dozens of hidden hawks took flight from the trees dotting the cliffs. They massed together at our rear, just as some of the biggest polecats and stoats emerged from secret places among the grasses and leaves. They didn't need much camouflage, but some looked as if they had rolled in the mud and covered themselves in leaves for good effect. The ranks of our enemies swelled, with almost an equal force gathered behind us as was in front.

'Never try to out-fox a fox, Guardian. The snare has been sprung and in the place of our choosing. I only regret that the Rabbit King himself didn't fall into our trap. Pity . . . but I guess the King is a trifle too soft and plump for an affair like this, isn't he?'

This insult prompted the suspended Tobin to take another swing with his foot, again nearly kicking one of his captors.

'If I can, I will make you eat those words, Fox!' he threatened while still whirling about helplessly.

'No, I'm afraid it's our time now . . . to eat you,' he said with a nod to a nearby hawk. 'Sound the attack.' Another loud cry pierced the air, and all our enemies started moving at once. The weasels began flowing like a tide over the bridge before us, while the polecats and stoats behind us pressed their advantage. The sound of battle cries mixed with ringing steel were heard all around. Screeching hawks dived in formation at our centre, only to be turned away by a quick evasion or the thrust of a pike. By the time the last of the stoats crossed the bridge to our bit of land, we were completely surrounded with our backs pressed to the river. The White Fox and his retinue were all that remained across the water from us. Over our shoulders now, we could hear their laughs and jeers, as we faced the foes pushing us closer and closer to the water's edge."

"With our backs to the river, the battle pressed in all around us now. The rabbits fought fiercely, as though their whole world depended on it, for so it did. One wave after another of weasel and stoat would charge up and then break upon shield and spear. The polecats took to using one another as living ramps to jump up and over the frontline defenders. These were met mostly by rabbit captains wielding swords, as spears were of less use in such close quarters. I struck one jumping polecat with my staff, knocking him into the water. As the river swept him away, he let out such a shriek that it gave the rest of the polecats a moment's pause. None of this, of course, escaped the watchful eye of the White Fox.

'Hawks, take the Guardian's staff and the day is won!' he shouted. From the sky, a chorus of voices answered back, 'The staff! The staff!'

From every direction, hawk after hawk now made a straight line for me—like dozens of bowlers taking aim at once for the same wicket. So, I did what any sporting lad would do in a similar situation who found a stick in his hand: I grasped it like a cricket bat and began to swing away. I made a few solid connections too, before the unexpected happened.

I remember swinging high and hard over my head, narrowly missing a diving hawk. On the down stroke, the head of my staff struck the river—but not with the small sound of a splash that I expected. It was more like the sudden roar of a hundred waterfalls bursting to life! From where the staff first hit, water exploded outwards in every direction. Most of the diving hawks were immediately engulfed and brought down, feathers drenched. The White Fox and his guards on the other side of the river were also wet from ear to tail. Even those of our enemies who didn't find themselves suddenly soaked stopped their attack and stood still for a moment in wonder.

'Holy Moses!' I exclaimed. Incredibly, the flow

of the river in front of me had come to a stop, and now between us and the White Fox stood only the smooth stones of the riverbed. The Fox and I locked eyes for a moment and I could see the first seeds of doubt taking root behind his astonished gaze.

'Quick across!' I shouted to the rabbits.

'And hold the bridge against them!' added Tobin from across the river. Tobin's shocked and dripping captors had let him fall to the ground. Though still bound, he regained his feet and was already well out of their reach now and barking commands.

The rabbit army flooded across the newly-made road in the river. For whatever reason, neither weasel, stoat nor polecat dared to pursue. Perhaps even that terrible company were taught their ancient history better than some children I know? As the last rabbit foot left the riverbed floor, the river broke forth again with renewed force. Had any of our enemies followed they would've surely been swept off and drowned by such a current.

'Spearmen to the bridge, and hold fast!' Tobin

commanded. 'The day isn't ours yet.'

'Indeed, it is not!' spoke a harsh voice in return. The White Fox and his personal guard were now surrounded and cut off from their army, but his old confidence was returning as he spoke. 'You've changed sides of the river, but you haven't changed the odds of the fight—however clever and impressive your little trick may have been. The bridge still stands and you cannot hold it forever against the determined alliance of all your foes. Your hope is still a lost one!'

'No! Hope lives yet!' came a high-pitched voice from above, but it wasn't the squawk of a hawk. Away up on the ridge, atop a crumbling tower of hewn stone, the Venerable Archibald suddenly appeared with a monocle in his eye and a golden horn in his hands.

'Hope lives, for the King comes!' With those words, Archibald blew on the great horn, producing a sound far louder than any horn blown by such a thin rabbit ever had the right to make.

At first nothing happened. But just when you began to believe nothing ever would happen, a sudden tremor ran through the ground. The sounds of distant *thuds* were heard and could be felt drawing nearer. Then, crowning the hill like help beyond hope, a majestic stag appeared flashing his great antlers. The entire herd of the Studley Royal Deer Park was at his heels. Upon the lordly stag's back sat the Rabbit King, clothed for war and clutching a silver spear.

'The battle looks quite heated down there in the valley,' the Rabbit King said to the Stag. 'Shall we join in, my old friend?'

'Yes, and may the old alliances be renewed,' the Lord Stag replied.

In that moment, the cry went up among the herd atop the hill, 'For the King's Warren!' In return the rabbits down in the valley took up the call, 'And for the Royal Deer!'

'Charge!' commanded the Lord Stag, and the rest of his herd followed him—nearly a hundred strong. They bounded down the steep hill like . . .

uh . . . well . . . like deer. The enemy now trapped on the other side of the river wailed in their dismay. Some threw down their weapons and attempted to flee. Others were trampled down and driven back into the river. None were allowed to cross the bridge now held resolutely by the rabbit pikemen. A cheer went up, "*Huzzah!*" each time another weasel or stoat was knocked into the river and swept away from the battlefield.

'Victory! Victory is ours!' the Rabbit King took up the call, raising high his silver spear.

'NOT YET!' came an angry voice behind me. In our wonder and joy, we had forgotten all about the White Fox. Before I could turn around, the fox came charging at me full of fury. I felt the sudden pain of steel claws ripping into my back as he barrelled into me, knocking me off balance and then to the ground. My helmet went flying off and my staff fell from my hand, landing just out of reach. When I looked up, the White Fox stared at me through vengeful eyes with teeth bared.

'This battle may be lost, Guardian, but . . . so are you!' he said as he lunged for my throat.

'NOOOO!' came a cry in return. But it didn't come from me. It came from Tobin as he threw himself in a single leap between the fox's open mouth and what ought to have been my death.

'*Crack!*' came the awful noise. Horrified, I realised it was the sound of Tobin's neck breaking, as the White Fox flung him aside with his deadly jaws. The fox looked on with satisfaction for half a moment at the knight's lifeless body before readying himself for another kill.

'*CRACK!*' came another awful sound. But this time it was the sound of my staff breaking over the fox's head. On the very spot where he had stood gloating, the White Fox fell to the ground—never to rise again.

A sudden stillness settled over the battlefield. The Royal Stag bearing the Rabbit King crossed the bridge amid the silence. He stopped at the place where Tobin lay. As the Stag lowered his head in respect, the Rabbit King descended regally down the deer's neck, between his wide antlers.

As the King's foot touched the ground, every head around bowed. There was a visible sadness in his eyes as the King looked down upon Tobin.

'Truly, he was the bravest of my knights,' the Rabbit King said now standing beside me.

'He gave his life to save mine,' I said.

'The noblest sacrifice that a friend could make.'

'Yes, it was,' I replied, feeling in that moment the deep gratefulness that only those delivered from a violent death can ever feel.

'Bear him up, Rabbits of the Warren!' the King called out. 'Sir Tobin shall have an honour guard for his return trip home.'

In very short work, many of the abandoned shields and spears were fashioned by nimble rabbit paws into a funeral bier. With my own two hands, I picked up Tobin and laid him upon the shields of his enemies. I covered his lifeless body with the White Fox's own crimson cloak. Eight of the Rabbit King's royal guards lifted the bier onto their shoulders and began to slowly carry him away.

'Wait!' I said, not wanting to let him leave. 'He would want his own sword to go with him.'

With tears blurring my vision, I searched the

battlefield for Tobin's sword but could not find it anywhere. In my search, however, my eyes did fall upon my broken staff. The rod of almond wood had broken in two. From the splintered ends of each piece, the magical blue glow could be seen slowly seeping out—as though the staff's lifeblood were spilling onto the ground. Even as I watched, the flow gave signs of fading. The power in the staff was dying as well.

'Over here,' I said holding up both pieces. The broken staff resembled two blue torches in my hands—torches that were quickly going out.

'Tobin should be carried home with these across his chest.'

As I added the Guardian's staff to the funeral bier, something of a 'last goodbye' began to slip out—much like those thoughts you never meant to speak aloud but, to your own surprise, they just started pouring out of you like air from a punctured tyre.

'My dear Tobin. You were the one who first found me. You guided and befriended me. You believed in me, when I didn't know what to believe. You brought me to this staff. It's fitting that this staff now goes with you.' I wrapped Tobin's lifeless paws around the broken bits.

'Farewell, my friend, you were . . . *what in the* . . . OH MY!'

At that very moment, the last bit of blue light burst from the broken staff—like the delayed explosion of a firecracker. Accompanying this unexpected blast, there was also the sudden *click* of bone upon bone. All that remained of the staff's blue magic, which for a moment hung like smoke about Tobin's face, rushed into his small nostrils and disappeared forever.

A mighty intake of breath quickly gave way to the heartiest laugh that ears have ever heard. Clear-eyed, Tobin sat up with a jolt upon his own funeral bier—which, in astonishment, several of the King's guards promptly dropped. This sent Tobin rolling head over tail onto the ground. He continued to laugh with every roll.

Until you've experienced something so incredibly good and unexpected, you've no idea how natural it is to laugh. It was contagious—like the most solemn of ceremonies had only been the prelude for a good joke which everyone found funny all at once. Laughing myself, I ran to Tobin and embraced him. Whatever duty and decorum that is owed to knights was forgotten in that moment. There we hugged like long-lost friends. Like brothers-in-arms meeting when the final victory has been won.

'Bless my soul!' said Archibald, now standing at our side and gazing through his monocle at the broken staff. 'There must have been a little magic left yet in that old staff you found.'

'Yes!' I said through a smile that would not go away. 'And I could not imagine a better way to spend it!'

'Nor I!' said the King. 'The Guardian's staff parted things while it was whole. Now, while smashed to bits, its final act pulled broken things back together again. A fitting end, I'll say. All of the old magic eventually comes to an end, you know. But friendship,' the King said with a wink of his eye, 'that is a deeper magic still—one that not even Death itself can kill.'

'You speak words both wise and true,' said the Lord Stag. 'Now, as one last token of our royal friendship, allow my people to bear all of your brave folk up in honour and carry you to the edge of our realm.'

'Gladly!' the Rabbit King answered. Then at the King's command, beginning with the wounded, every warrior mounted a deer. Some carried as many as five or six rabbits on their backs with every spear lifted and banner flying. I mounted a large stag, who laughed as I put my helmet back on ("Too bad you're stuck with ears instead of antlers," he joked).

Tobin joined me on the stag's back, as the whole herd moved off together as one. We bounded down the valley and over green hills, through the wooded parkland and down tree-lined lanes. You may have ridden a horse before, but a horse is nothing compared to the thrill of riding a deer. It's like gliding over the land on a giant grasshopper with horns. The thrill of that first ride will ever live in my memory.

On the edge of Studley Roger, we said a merry

goodbye to the Stag King and his large herd. Every royal deer reared and waved their front hooves from the hilltop, as we shouted our last farewell and began the journey home.

That night was like no other in the Halls of the Rabbit King. The taste of victory was still sweet upon our lips, which only made the taste of everything else that much sweeter. There were toasts to drink, good food to eat, and dances to join in. That was the beginning of my life as a Guardian and the greatest season of peace that the King's Warren has ever known."

"But the peace didn't last forever, did it?" Michael interrupted. Up until now, the two of us had been content only to listen to Old Sam's story.

"Aye," said Sam. He grimaced a little as he readjusted himself on the sofa. "The peace was not to last, sadly. We do not yet live in a world where a peace can last forever. For now, at least, the fight is never truly over. More battles were certainly to come."

"Like when we found you by the Arrows this evening? Facedown and covered in cuts?"

"Yes . . . but that's a story for another day. And, lads, there's a lifetime of stories between my first battle and today's fight. Come again tomorrow, and we'll see what other adventures I feel like retelling." Ol' Sam gave us a weak smile as he set down his finished cup of tea, his tale finally told.

"Ahhh! Yorkshire Tea, that's a proper brew, that is! Fix me one last cuppa, if you please, and then you two ought to be off home."

Michael put the kettle on again, as I helped the old man off with his wellies and propped up his socked feet on the sofa. This same sofa also served as the only bed in the one-room house. Before placing a fresh cup of tea in his shaky hands, I covered him over with a patchwork blanket.

"Alright, how's that? Michael and I will pop back round tomorrow. Please, may we hear another story then?"

Sam made no answer but gave a contented smile in return. He closed his eyes and pulled the blanket up to his neck as we said our goodbyes. We shut the door promising that we would be back as soon as we could the next day.

We did go back the next day . . . and the day after that . . . and the day after that. But Old Sam wasn't there. He wasn't in his house. He wasn't at the Arrows. He wasn't anywhere to be found. Believe me, we looked and looked!

We began asking around the town after him, but no one had seen him about. It was all very baffling to us Boroughbridgians. In a week's time, he was a missing person. In twenty years' time, he is still a missing person as well as a local unsolved mystery.

"Whatever happened to Ol' Daft Sam?" someone would ask.

"Maybe the fairies took him, so often he was away with them?" someone might answer.

"Away with the fairies?" I'd say to Michael. "More like he was the only one who saw things straight. Let's go have another look." And then Michael and I would go out again to the place people wrongly associate with the Devil.

Day by day and year by year, the two of us would return to *The Rabbit's Arrows*—that's their true name, remember. We would go out and look again, hoping to discover the Ley Line marked by those ancient stones. We always went at sunset and always went expecting that something incredible could happen.

"Maybe this is the correct path?" we would guess.

"Maybe today is the right day? Maybe we'll stumble upon it if we just try one more time?"

I'm sad to say that we never got it quite right. We were never fortunate enough to receive *the Sight* so as to see the world as it really is—with animals that talk and rabbits that carry swords.

But maybe . . . just maybe . . . we failed because we always went expecting. Perhaps the magic only happens when it's least expected. Or, maybe, it's not yet time for another Guardian. I don't know.

What I do know is this: every time I walk the Ley Line at sunset, the rabbits are there . . . and they are watching.

READ-ALOUD ADVENTURES

MEET THE TEAM

THE AUTHOR

K.J. Pugh is an American who spent most of his 30s sojourning in Europe with his wife and two lovely kids. He enjoys walking, cycling, consuming cups of Yorkshire Tea, as well as inserting quotes from J.R.R. Tolkien and C.S. Lewis into casual conversations.

In the spring of 2021, K.J. returned from France to his native Alabama in order to pastor his home church, Alberta Baptist, in Tuscaloosa.

(www.AlbertaBaptist.org)

THE ILLUSTRATOR

Andrew Bosley is a freelance illustrator and owner of Wits End Studios. He lives in northern Arizona with his wife and five kids. He has a ukulele hanging on his wall, so he thinks he can play it. But he really can't.

(www.BosleyArt.com)

THE GRAPHIC ARTIST

Dann May is an Australian visual artist and game developer with a lifelong love for imaginative worlds and tabletop games. He created the graphic design for beautiful board games like *Everdell* and *A War of Whispers*. Together with his wife and brother, Dann founded Quillsilver Studio in 2020.

(www.Quillsilver.com)

THE AUDIOBOOK NARRATOR

Michael J Tinker is a Somerset-based singer, songwriter and performer.
As well as releasing numerous albums and performing shows around the UK,
he has also lent his voice/accent talent to recording various audiobooks.
He loves playing cricket, dabbling in the world of leathercraft,
and producing the TV series *Adventures of the Juniper.*

(www.MichaelJTinker.com)

THE AUDIOBOOK MUSICIAN

Nicholas Alexander composed and produced the original musical score for the audiobook. He lives in Brixton, London, with his collection of road bikes, and he spends his spare time racing his friends up South London's steepest hills.

(www.NocholasAlexander.org)

THE EDITOR

Jo Tinker is a freelance proofreader and also the Finance Manager for Contagious Bible Ministries. She lives in Somerset with her husband, three children and dog Leeli, and loves walking in the Quantock Hills, exploring England's South West coastline, and curling up in front of the fire with a good book.

PROJECT PATRONS

Mike DePasquale
Tom Allen
Stephen & Caitlin Bowles
Cecil & Jane Lancaster
Stephen Webb
James Wilson
Chloe & Lilly Parchman
J. Kameron Pugh
The Lowes
The Kizziah Crew
Joel Runge
The Thompsons
Kyle & Hayley Bryant
Parker Windle
B.A.I.G.M.D.
Katherine Selman
Ben & Tara Robinson
Mark Phillippo
The Geis Family
Cindy
Susan Morgan Skelton
Mama T
Dan Jarnigan
Benjamin Johnson
Matthew & Katie Richardson
Matthew Andrews
Lanny & Donna Holbrook
Allen Parker
Liza Galloway
Theresa Melton
David & Katie Sullivan
The Ross Family
Jim Winter
Caleb Klontz
Jim & Lisa
Gheorghe Orbesteanu
Daniel Wolf
Anonymous

Your kind generosity brought *The Rabbit's Arrows* to life and made the book better for everyone. Thank you so much!

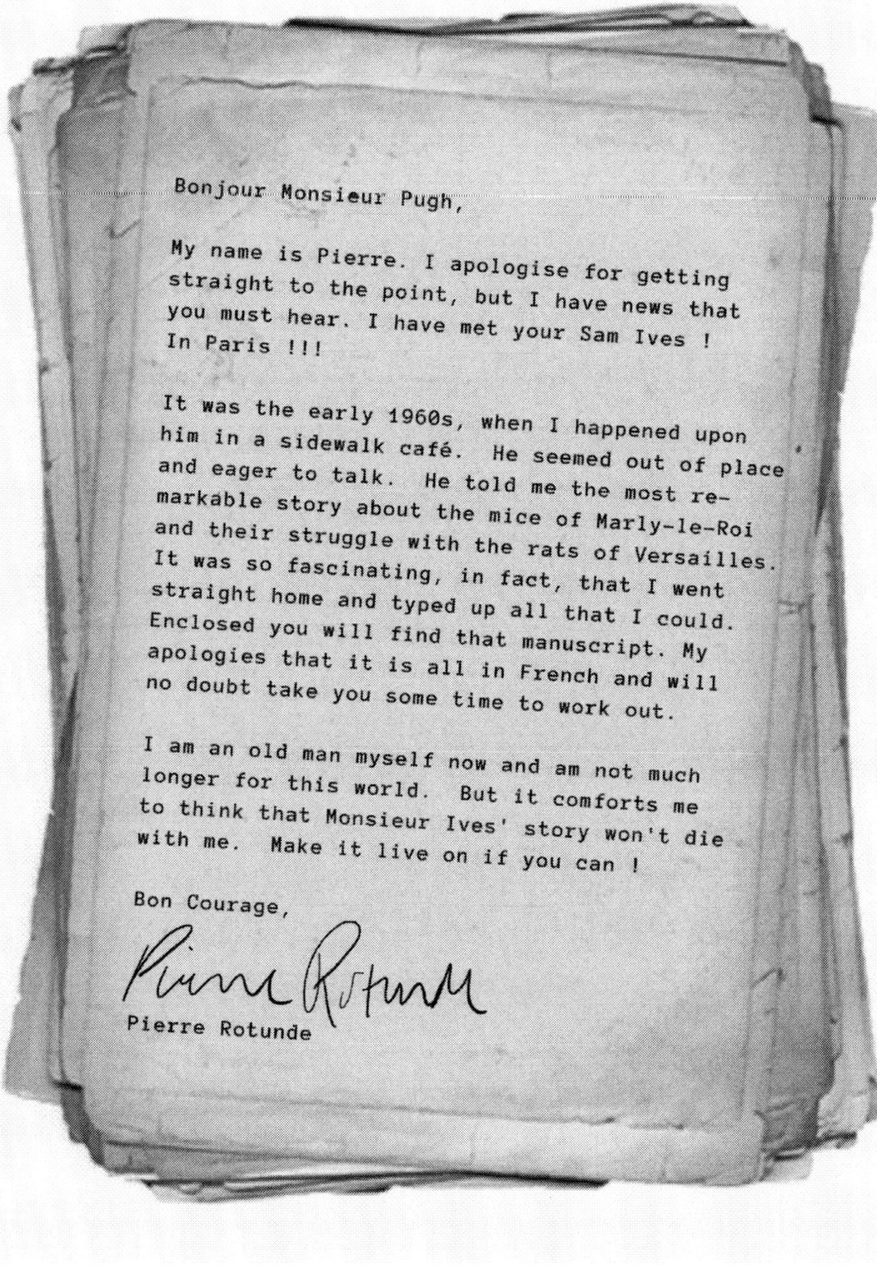

Bonjour Monsieur Pugh,

My name is Pierre. I apologise for getting straight to the point, but I have news that you must hear. I have met your Sam Ives ! In Paris !!!

It was the early 1960s, when I happened upon him in a sidewalk café. He seemed out of place and eager to talk. He told me the most remarkable story about the mice of Marly-le-Roi and their struggle with the rats of Versailles. It was so fascinating, in fact, that I went straight home and typed up all that I could. Enclosed you will find that manuscript. My apologies that it is all in French and will no doubt take you some time to work out.

I am an old man myself now and am not much longer for this world. But it comforts me to think that Monsieur Ives' story won't die with me. Make it live on if you can !

Bon Courage,

Pierre Rotunde

Printed in Poland
by Amazon Fulfillment
Poland Sp. z o.o., Wrocław
16 December 2021

073d59c4-bf72-47b4-a265-ceee1dce8469R02